L.F. Ant

Written by Michael Hedman
Illustrated by Peter Jadoonath

atmosphere press

Dedicated to my wife and children for their motivation and patience, and to D.S. from the CMS library for her belief and inspiration.
Thank You!

They say it's a small world. Definitely true for ants. Especially true for me. How small am I? Knee-high to a grasshopper? Nope. Knee-high to an ant? Not even that. Now get this, my name is Lawrence Fredrick Ant. For short (yes, I know, a short joke!), I go by Larry Fred. Even shorter than that, my best friend just calls me L.F.

I'm L.F. Ant. Do you get it? (don't worry, you will)

I'm not too happy about my situation. I'm self-conscious about it.

I get teased about it. "Little Larry" they call me. I hate being small! I have a bit of chip on my shoulder because of it (well, more of a chip *crumb*!).

I do have one friend, my best friend, who never brings up my size. Is he another ant? No, that would be too obvious. My BFF is O-double-E. "One-Eye" Ed. He is an elephant. (Now do you get it?) Oh, the irony!

They call him One-Eye because he wears an eye patch. He was born partially blind in one eye.

He's not happy about his situation. He' self-conscious about it. He gets teased for wearing it. He's the only elephant who has one. He hates that eye patch! He avoids wearing it whenever he can.

I wish I was like him, though. What it must feel like to be that BIG and POWERFUL! For one day I could be king of the anthill! Imagine that, I wouldn't have to worry about wind gusts, raindrops, being stepped on, or anything. I just want to feel normal!

Ed wishes he had perfect vision like me, though. What it must feel like to see everything clearly! For one day, he wouldn't have to worry about depth-perception, blurry images, bumping into trees, or anything. He just wants to feel normal!

Well, get this. On a hot, summer day we decided to take a swim in the nearby mountain stream to cool off. When I meet up with Ed on the forest path through our village, he wasn't wearing his eye patch. Instead, he was wearing eyeglasses!

"Hey, Ed, are those new?" I asked. "They look pretty cool on you."

"Yeah, they are new, thanks. They're supposed to help my blind eye, but I don't like them at all!" Ed replied, pushing up his glasses. "They keep slipping and sliding off my trunk. They won't stay in place. I can't see anything with these! I think there's a piece that's broken, but I can't tell because everything is so small."

"Do you want me to take a look at them? Remember, Little is the name, Small is the game!" I joked.

Ed chuckled. "Sure, check them out," he said, as he set them down on the ground.

Being the mini-ant I am, I was able to wiggle and wriggle and move and maneuver into and around all the little screws and hinges and loops. With my little mandibles and antennae, I tightened and loosened and shifted and turned several parts and pieces.

When I was done, he tried them on. They didn't slip or slide.

"Hey, you fixed them! Thanks, L.F. I can see a lot better now!" Ed exclaimed.

Amazed at the clarity and detail his newly repaired glasses provided, Ed gazed around in awe at his forest surroundings. Then suddenly, Ed hollered out.

"L.F. look! Something is coming at us!"

In a flash, he scooped me up with his trunk and set me on his back. I peered up at the mountain, squinting with all my might, but I did not notice anything.

"What is it, Ed? I don't see anything. What's wrong?" I asked.

Ed didn't say anything, he just spun around so fast I almost fell off. He started running through the forest, trumpeting warning calls to his herd. When I looked back, I saw it; an avalanche of boulders and mud and clouds of dust, gaining momentum and ready to swallow us up whole! Clinging onto my fearless friend for dear life, I had never been more frightened. But Ed was fast, and he was able to outrun the downpour of debris.

With speed and adrenaline, we made it back to Ed's herd. He warned them of the oncoming danger. The avalanche was approaching rapidly, destroying and tearing everything in its path. Just in time, the herd all moved to the safety of higher ground, but we had to keep going. Panting and struggling for strength, Ed kept pace ahead of the torrent of wreckage.

With no time to spare, we made it to the anthills. I shouted and screamed and directed the colony to hide and take cover. They scurried and hurried and acted quickly, finding shelter inside the hills. Although their sand-pile homes were mostly ruined, all the ants would be able to emerge safely from under the rubble afterward.

A little further down the path, Ed finally veered off toward the safety of a high ridge. Falling to the ground in exhaustion, we watched the avalanche pass. Both of us sitting there silently in shock, thinking about what had just happened, I was finally able to speak.

"Whew, Ed! That was so close! You saved us! Good thing you had your glasses on. I didn't see anything."

"I sure am glad I had them on, and you were able to fix them. It's a good thing you were small enough to make the repairs. If not, well, I don't want to think about what would have happened," Ed acknowledged, still trying to catch his breath.

We thought about what we had said. "Good" and "small" in the same sentence? "Good" and "glasses" in the same sentence? We were smiling and beaming with pride! We had done something important. We saved our friends and family. Back home they would call us heroes, throw us parades, and maybe even give us a key to the village!

I guess we learned a lesson from all that. I'm small, but that's cool. Ed needs glasses, and that's cool, too. It's not a bad thing. We are fine with it. What others might think and say doesn't really matter.

Now everything is pretty much back to normal. I mean, I'm still Little Larry, but I don't mind. Ed still has his glasses. But Ed has a new nickname. He's no longer known as One-Eye. No, my BFF is now F-double-E. "Four-Eyes" Ed. And he LOVES it!

A few days later we met up again along the path.

"Hey, L.F., finally ready for that swim now?" Ed asked.

"Can't wait! You have your glasses?" I asked.

Ed looked at me and smiled. "Nope. Check these out," he held up something I had never seen before, "prescription swimming goggles!"

"Super-Cool! What a great *eye*-dea!" I said as I winked. We both laughed!

It may be a small world, but *clearly*, being a *little* different in it is okay!

About the Author

Michael's love for writing and rhyming and all things words started a long time ago at a small, corner desk in a bedroom far, far away. Since those days, Michael grew up and became a professional baseball player, vacuum salesman, waiter, marathoner, and 5th grade teacher. Rumored to once have been a Secret Service agent, he keeps a low profile and his appearance mysterious. (However, that has never been verified.) Standing 6'6", he may be the world's tallest children's book author. (That, also, has never been verified). On any given day, you might find him on the golf course, tennis court, or basketball blacktop trying to stay active. Never taking himself too seriously, Michael works, coaches, and lives in NW Indiana with his wife, three children, and three cats.

About the Illustrator

Peter and his family live in Minnesota. There, he makes pottery, draws pictures with his kids, chases chickens, and barbecues with friends. Peter and the author, Mike, were high school buddies back in the day. They were always joking around, trading baseball cards, playing catch, and playing basketball. Although they drifted apart, the creation of L.F. Ant gave the two of them the opportunity to reunite. In many ways, the story of Ed and Larry resembles Peter and Mike's own friendship.

About Atmosphere Press

Atmosphere Press is an independent, full-service publisher for excellent books in all genres and for all audiences. Learn more about what we do at atmospherepress.com.

We encourage you to check out some of Atmosphere's latest releases, which are available at Amazon.com and via order from your local bookstore:

Gloppy, by Janice Laakko
Wildly Perfect, by Brooke McMahan
How Grizzly Found Gratitude, by Dennis Mathew
Do Lions Cry?, by Erina White
Sadie and Charley Finding Their Way, by Bonnie Griesemer
Silly Sam and the Invisible Jinni, by Shayla Emran Bajalia
Feeling My Feelings, by Shilpi Mahajan
Zombie Mombie Saves the Day, by Kelly Lucero
The Fable King, by Sarah Philpot
Blue Goggles for Lizzy, by Amanda Cumbey
Neville and the Adventure to Cricket Creek, by Juliana Houston
Peculiar Pets: A Collection of Exotic and Quixotic Animal Poems, by Kerry Cramer
Carlito the Bat Learns to Trick-or-Treat, by Michele Lizet Flores
Zoo Dance Party, by Joshua Mutters
Beau Wants to Know, a picture book by Brian Sullivan
The King's Drapes, a picture book by Jocelyn Tambascio
You are the Moon, a picture book by Shana Rachel Diot
Onionhead, a picture book by Gary Ziskovsky
Odo and the Stranger, a picture book by Mark Johnson
Jack and the Lean Stalk, a picture book by Raven Howell
Brave Little Donkey, a picture book by Rachel L. Pieper
Buried Treasure: A Cool Kids Adventure, a picture book by Anne Krebbs

CPSIA information can be obtained
at www.ICGtesting.com
Printed in the USA
LVHW070840140122
708388LV00007B/210